KT-513-267

2 2 AU

Books should be returned or renewed by the last
date above. Renew by phone **03000 41 31 31** or
online *www.kent.gov.uk/libs*

_____

_____

CUSTOMER
SERVICE
EXCELLENCE

**Kent
County
Council**
kent.gov.uk

ibraries Registration & Archives

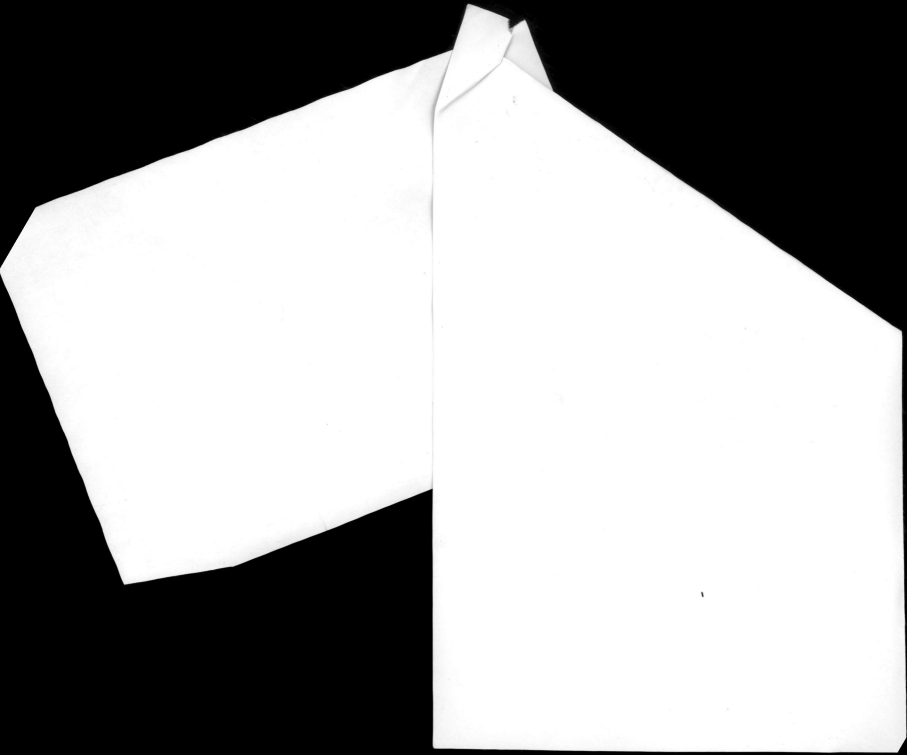

Archie and George and the New Bikes

There are lots of Early Reader
stories you might enjoy.

Look at the back of the book or,
for a complete list, visit
www.orionchildrensbooks.co.uk

Archie and George and the New Bikes

James Brown

Orion
Children's Books

ORION CHILDREN'S BOOKS

First published in Great Britain in 2016 by Hodder and Stoughton

1 3 5 7 9 10 8 6 4 2

A CIP catalogue record for this book
is available from the British Library.

ISBN 978 1 4440 1529 4

Printed and bound in China

The paper and board used in this book are from well-managed forests
and other responsible sources.

Orion Children's Books
An imprint of
Hachette Children's Group
Part of Hodder and Stoughton
Carmelite House
50 Victoria Embankment
London EC4Y 0DZ

An Hachette UK Company

www.hachette.co.uk
www.hachettechildrens.co.uk

*For Grandad, the kindest man
I know, and Grandma, who was
my best critic – J.B.*

Contents

Chapter One

This is Archie Thomas Smith.
He likes to be called Archie.

And this is George Andrew Smith. He likes to be called George.

But George does not like to be
called Archie. And Archie does
not like to be called George.

Whatever you do, don't get
their names wrong.

Archie and George are
identical twins. Archie is six
minutes older than George.

Their big sister Maddy can always tell them apart. She never gets them mixed up.

Archie and George may look the same but they are very different.

Archie loves ball games and running.

George loves drawing and reading.

But Archie and George agree on one thing. Their favourite times are when Grandma and Grandad come to visit.

Chapter Two

One day Grandma and Grandad came over for tea.

George was finishing a
picture for Maddy's birthday.
Archie was drawing too but
he was not happy. He didn't like
his picture. It was all wrong.

"Maybe this will cheer you up," said Grandad, handing Archie a plastic bag.

"And this one's for you," said Grandma to George.

They looked inside. Each of them had a new helmet.

"But we don't have bikes," said Archie.

"You do now!" smiled Grandad. "Last one outside is a rotten egg."

Archie jumped up, knocking
crayons everywhere.

"WOW! A bike!" he screamed,
following Grandma and Grandad.

George watched Archie go.
There was no point in running.
Archie always got there first!

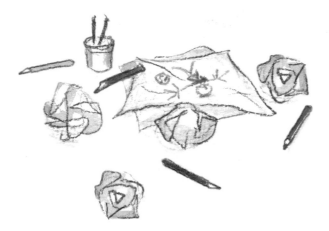

Chapter Three

George went outside and saw
his new bike.

"What do you say to
Grandma and Grandad?"
asked Mum.

George tried to smile.
"Thank you," he said.

Archie was already riding around the garden.

"Well done, Archie! Keep pedalling," Grandad cheered. "Soon you'll be able to ride without stabilisers!"

"What are stabilisers?" George asked.

"The extra wheels," Grandma said, clipping George's helmet on. "They keep you steady until you can ride without them. Come on, your turn."

They wheeled his green bike
to the top of the garden.

"Hop on," Grandma said.
"I've got you, don't worry."

George felt very wobbly. His feet couldn't touch the floor and his helmet felt too tight.

He had a feeling something bad was going to happen.

Chapter Four

George tried and tried. He
wanted to pedal smoothly
so he wouldn't fall off.

But it was no
good. He kept
swerving into
the flowers

or falling off
sideways.

"It's lucky you've got
a helmet!" Grandad called.

Archie was now riding
in circles around the garden.

He didn't even need
Grandad's help.

George was fed up. "I can't do it!" he said.

"Yes you can, George!" Grandma said, "You've nearly got it. One more try."

"Let's race!" said Archie.
"Ready? Set. Go!"

Archie shot off. George did too.
He was doing it! He was riding!

George forgot to look where he was going.

"The pond!" cried Grandad. "The Pond!"

But it was too late.

George landed **splash** straight into the pond. He was covered in frogspawn and slimy pondweed.

Archie couldn't stop laughing.
"You look like a frog!"

Chapter Five

Before long Archie could ride
all by himself. He didn't even
need stabilisers. George's bike
was still in the shed.

"Archie!" Dad called. "It's time to go."

Archie was very excited. He was going with Dad and Grandad to a football match.

Maddy was going to ballet
with Mum and George was
painting a picture.

When the others had all gone, Grandma said "Why don't we ride to the park?"

"Can we have some ice cream?" George asked.

"Of course," Grandma said.

"Will I have to ride my bike?" asked George.

Grandma nodded. "Practice makes perfect," she said. "It'll be fun."

Chapter Six

There were lots of people at the park walking their dogs, eating picnics, flying kites or going for a run.

At first George was very
wobbly.

He fell
over
a lot.

But before they knew it George could stay on without Grandma's help. Soon they were riding side by side.

George couldn't stop smiling.

And he couldn't stop pedalling!

The best bit was zooming down the hill.

"See," Grandma said as she handed George his ice cream. "I knew you could do it. It just takes a bit of practice."

"Thank you, Grandma," George said. "And thank you for the ice cream too."

Chapter Seven

When George got home he
was out of breath. He had grass
stains on his knees and a big
smile on his face.

Archie, Maddy, Grandad, Dad and Mum were eating dinner.

"Where have you two been?" asked Mum.

"We've been to the park!"
George said.

"And we've got a surprise for
you," said Grandma. "Come
and see!"

George got on to his bike and
whizzed around the garden.
"I can ride! Without stabilisers!"

"I've got a surprise for you too," Archie said, running inside. When he came back out he was carrying a card.

"Sorry I laughed at you,"
Archie said. "I drew it myself."
   On the front was a picture
of George on a green bike and
Archie on a red bike.

And inside was the funniest
picture George had ever seen.

"Next time let's ride our bikes together," Archie said.

"Okay," said George, "but you'll have to keep up."

What are you going to read next?

Don't miss Archie and George's next story about the **Christmas Show**.

If you like **Archie and George**, you'll also enjoy **Lottie and Dottie**, who grow their own **carrots** and **sunflowers** and **pumpkins**,

football adventures in **Albert and the Garden of Doom,**

and Timothy making a special mud pie in **Chocolate Porridge.**